SURVIVING THE APOCALYPSE

ASTHA THAKOR

To my mum and dad, without them, this book would never have been published. And to my middle school english teacher without whom, this book would not exist.Thank you to everyone who contributed towards the making of this book. And thank you for criticising it, for without that, I would never be motivated enough to keep going and reach here. AND FINALLY TO MY PAST SELF, without her too, my book wouldn't exist.

Contents

Foreword

Most of the incidences occured in this book, are a figment of my unrealistic imagination. This book had started out as a mere school project, then expanded to a hand-written book and then halfway through turned into an e-book. And finally after a year and a half, it is published on paper.

Acknowledgements

I would like to say that this book is the brainchild of my imagination and the starting line of a mere story for a school project. I would like to acknowledge Rekha Bhattacharya ma'am(my middle school teacher) for igniting this spark of imagination inside my mind. Thanks, mum, dad, my Nana, Nani, Dada, Dadi, all my uncles and aunts for always congratulating and encouraging me. I would like to acknowledge Rudra, my brother for being my best criticiser and always being the first one to read my stories. Thanks to my high school english teacher, Jasmine ma'am, for encouraging me to keep going. And the last acknowledgement for my real friends who were always happy for me.

Preface

Do you see that girl running? The one wearing a grey tee and black ripped jeans and a black jacket, with a medium skin tone, heart shape freckled face, small button, sad round brown eyes, thin, arched eyebrows, soft, pink rosebud lips? No? See there? That short one? Yes? Her. The one with a slim build, and wavy, medium-length auburn brown hair? That is Elizabeth Lewis.

I am Elizabeth Lewis. You can call me Liz. I was born on 2nd September 2016 Winterville. I am 17. I study at Woodlane junior high school. When I was 7, my parents said they were leaving for a business trip. They never came back. I lived in an orphanage until I was 10. I did not like it there. All the kids used to bully and beat me. One day I made an excuse of going to the market... and escaped. I bumped into Tom while running. He was still studying but lived alone. Tom's parents and my parents were business partners. T Tom recognized me immediately. He took me to his house and phoned his parents. They came there in about 10 minutes. They realized what had happened. hey had searched for me but I could not be found. They thought that my mum and dad had taken me with them and that I was also dead.After thinking for a while, they decided that they would adopt me. They raised me like I was their own daughter. I had a family. Loving and caring parents, and a protective brother. And I was going to Woodlane junior high school. That is where I met him during chemistry class. I was paired with him for a project. I thought we would become good friends. And we did. Not good but best friends. I introduced him to Tom. And before we knew it, all three of us were hanging out all the time. And now I am studying with Tristan in Woodlane junior high.

Do you see that guy walking? The one wearing a beige hoodie and blue pants? With a fair skin tone, triangular face, emotionless sapphire blue eyes, thick dark eyebrows, thin, flat lips? The one with an athletic build, and short wavy chestnut brown hair? That one who's got an outstanding height? That is Thomas Henderson.

I am Thomas Henderson. AKA Tom. I was born on 15th May 2014 in Winterville. I am 19. I study at Woodlane high school. Once when I walking to school, I bumped into a girl. She looked up to me, straight into my eyes. I recognized her immediately. I took her home and phoned my parents. They told her what had happened after her parents left. They thought for some time, and then decided that they would adopt her. Soon after, Liz started studying at Woodlane junior high. She met Tristan there. She introduced him to me. And a few days later, we didn't even realize that we were hanging out together all the time.

Inside the chemistry lab ,Woodlane junior high.

Do you see that guy wearing a white tee and black denim jacket with jeans? The one with a fair skin tone, diamond shaped face, soft ash gray eyes, straight eyebrows, thin lips? The one with the toned body. No? The one with dark brown, neck-length wavy hair? See there, the one sitting beside Liz. Yes. That guy is Tristan Hillary.

I am Tristan Hillary. A. K. A Tris. I was born on 31st July 2016 in Winterville. I am 17. I too study at Woodlane junior high school. In the 2nd week of school, a new student entered our class. The teacher introduced the student. It was Liz. Afterwards, during chemistry class, we were paired together for a project. The conversation started with an awkward hello. For project work we had to meet every day for about a week. We started to get comfortable around each other. And after that, little did we realize, we started to hanging out together with Tom all the time.

Prologue

It was the year 2037. Elizabeth Lewis had rented a small house two streets Tristan's in Roguefield. Both of them had been working at Supernova. A corporation which focused on researching extra- terrestrial life. She was the head of the newest department which was searching for extra-terrestrial messages on the Moon. Tristan Hillary was in the Navigations department tracing the members of the Azura Station.Liz's elder brother Thomas Henderson worked as a model for 'Fiancy', a company which made luxurious jewellery for brides and grooms. A patient of the new COVID variant created chaos in their lives as a zombie apocalypse broke out in the world.

CHAPTER ONE

THE START

I woke up to a scream coming from the back of my house. I was scared, but I got out of bed, I opened the back door, and, to my horror, I saw Mrs. Welsh, my neighbor, being eaten by her husband, Mr. Welsh. I shouted, "Mr. Welsh! What in the world are you doing!?" Mr. Welsh turned to me. He didn't say anything. He groaned. There was blood all over his face. And his eyes had turned all white. He looked horrifying. I screamed and ran inside the house. I went into my room and took my phone. I heard screams for help outside my house. The screams were ghastly. I knew it wasn't safe to be here. I left my phone on the bed and took out a bag from my closet. I packed some of my clothes. I quickly went to my kitchen and grabbed a knife. I went to my room and opened the drawer beside my bed. I took my battery pack and charger out of it.

I took my phone from my bed and dialed Tom's number. He picked up and I whimpered, "Tom.... Tom, oh thank God! Tom, Mrs. Welsh..." and I couldn't speak. I started crying bitterly. "LIZ! Calm down! I know what is happening outside. Calm down, I am coming to take you. Don't come out of the house until I call you back. Okay?" he warned, taking a breath. "Okay." I said and cut the call. I grabbed my purse and put my battery pack and charger in it. I kept my bag over my shoulder in case Tom called, and I had to rush. I was about to call Tris when I heard a loud knock on my back door. "Open the door please! My sister is pregnant! Please!" The pleas turned into a scream. I was petrified. I remembered.... I ... I left the back door unlocked! I ran towards it. But it was too late. Mr. Welsh whom I had seen earlier was standing a few meters away from me. I was horrified. I turned the other way and ran. I grabbed my car keys and purse and hastily unlocked the main door.

I dashed towards my car. My hands were sweaty. I was fumbling around with the keys. The car wouldn't unlock. I was scared. I dropped the keys. SHIT. Those flesh-eating monsters were nearing me! I was panicking. "LIZ!? What in the world are you doing?!" shouted a familiar voice from behind me. I turned around and saw Tom in his car. "Tom! Thank God, finally!" I exclaimed, giving a sigh of relief. "Hop in! Come on!" Tom exclaimed. "Alright." I muttered, walking hastily towards his car.

I dumped my bag in the back seat and sat beside him in the front seat. He started to drive. Tom questioned, "Did I or did I not tell you not to come out of the house until I CALLED!" Tom was shouting at me for the first time. "Tom, look I know you are angry but... at least hear me out." I spoke, trying hard not to let my voice crack. "Okay, fine. And... I am sorry. Okay? I was just scared that something would happen to you." He apologized. I explained to him, everything that had happened back at the house. Tom and I didn't say anything to each other, all the way to Tris's house.He parked the car in a dark corner and explained, "I got a message from Tris about an hour ago. "He sounded a little scared, he said that there was a walker outside his house and that he needed help to get out." "Alright then, let me get my knife and we can go help Tris get out." I said taking out the knife from my bag. Tom looked at me and cleared himself, "Uh... no, you are not coming with me. I will go get Tris out and you will sit here. I saved you from getting yourself killed once and I don't want to do that again. Okay, Liz?" He stepped out of the car and from the trunk, he took out a wrench. He came back to my window, and I rolled it down. "Liz, look. Don't feel that I don't want you to come and save him. It's just that I care for you, and I don't want you to be somewhere unsafe. Okay lil' sister?" He joked. I showed him my knife and told him, "Call me little again and I will stab you." He chuckled and then he started walking away.

I waited and waited. Minutes passed and he returned. But the thing was, I could not see Tris with him. I got worried. I waited for him to sit back in the car and then questioned him angrily, "Tom! TELL ME WHAT IN THE WORLD HAPPENED TO TRISTAN! DID WE LOSE HIM?" As soon as I finished speaking, I broke down. Tom comforted me and, "LIZ! OH LORD, CALM DOWN! NOTHING HAS HAPPENED TO HIM. OH PLEASE! STOP CRYING FIRST AND SEE THIS NOTE! LOOK." I calmed down and Tom handed me a note. It looked as if it was written in a hurry. He had written:

MEET ME AT MILLBIRDS'! SEE YA THERE GUYS!
-TRIS

"Oh, good lord!" I breathed a sigh of relief. "So, our next stop is Millbird's, I guess." Tom giggled. "Yup. Let's go, Tom." I said looking out the window. And we were now on our way to the café to get Tristan. HOPEFULLY.

CHAPTER TWO

A New Hope

We reached Millbird's in about fifteen minutes. Tom parked the car under a tree. The sun was almost up. I looked at my watch. It was around five o'clock. I peered over Tom's shoulder and saw the sun rise. "Tom! Look!" I exclaimed, pointing towards the sun. "Yeah." Tom mumbled. Apparently, he wasn't interested in my talks. He was looking towards the rosewood door of the café. The one we used to go through every day. A log of wood was chained to the door handles. I shouted out loud, "Tristan! Tris!" Tom looked at me, "Liz. Go and stay in the car until I come to pick you up. Alright? Please?" Tom requested. "Okay. But I will come to save you if you land in trouble." I argued. "Yeah 'right." I heard Tom mumble under his breath. I started walking towards the car but turned halfway to Tom shouting, "LIZ! Look who we FINALLY found!" My eyes met the guy's eyes. Did I see them? I saw soft ash gray eyes looking at me. It had to be **him**. It had to be Tristan. No one looks at me like him. I closed my eyes, exhaled, and opened my eyes again. It was really him!

I ran towards him and pulled him into a tight hug, tears rolling down my face. "Oh my God! LIZ! Calm down!" Tris laughed. "Calm down!? We find you after four hours and you say *CALM DOWN!*" I sobbed. "Okay, stop crying. It's not like I am not dead or anything?!" He chuckled. "Yeah right." I said eyeing him. "Tris. Where the hell were you when we were shouting your name and searching for you ?!" Tom started questioning. "And why was the damn door *chained*?" I sensed an argument coming up. So, to cool down the heat I joked, "Alright Tom! Enough with the questions. Let the guy breathe at least." Tris started giggling. And I joined in. Tom smiled and joined in too. But suddenly, Tris heard a thud. He whispered, "Shh! Did you guys hear that?!" "WHAT!" I spoke in an irritated tone. And there was a thud again. I looked at the café door. It was as if... as if there was a... a hoard of walkers behind it. "TOM! LIZ!" "WE HAVE TO RUN!" Tris shouted. My thought bubble was broken.

A hoard of walkers was coming towards us. He grabbed my hand and ran towards the car. Tom was running right beside me. Tom opened the door and hastily sat in the driver's seat. Tristan shoved me in the back seat and sat beside Tom. He started driving fast. He was driving out of Shepherd Street. "Tom where are we going?!" "TOM!" I shouted. It was as if he wasn't listening. Suddenly he spoke up, "Yes! What?" "Where was your mind?" I muttered. "Look. We are going somewhere." He sighed. "I can see that. But where to?" I asked. He said, looking over the wheel, "Somewhere safe. Somewhere far away from this place. Someplace we can call home" We didn't speak a word to each other until Tom stopped the car after an hour.

We stopped in front of a house. It was in the middle of nowhere. The only patch of green was the backyard of the house. Tom looked at the house and sighed, "It isn't huge. But it's home." He got out of the car and went inside the house. Tris too got out but opened my door and sat beside me. I looked at him and asked, "Where were you? Where were you when we searched for you outside the café?" "I... I was... I was there. I saw you, Liz. I wanted to shout and say, 'I am here Liz, come and pull me into a hug like you always do.' But I couldn't. The truth is, when I escaped my apartment, I left a note for you then I came to your house, I... knocked several times... but no one came out. I was sure Tom would never leave you alone. He must have taken you because your car was still there. So, I made my way to the café. Mr. Miller was there. He... he told me that it wasn't safe to be outside the kitchen because the café door would break at any moment. I... I trusted him and went with him inside the kitchen. But then he showed his true colors. He hit my leg several times with a... a baseball bat, and I fell. Then he tied my legs and hands. I resisted hard. But because of the injury, I couldn't. He pushed me into a corner, and I heard him lock the door. I immediately started trying to figure out how to get out. Suddenly I heard a growl. It was coming from the other corner. I squinched my eyes, and... and saw Mrs. Miller. Her eyes were blank! I freaked out. She suddenly jumped on me. I was trying to resist her... and then suddenly... suddenly I heard you Liz... I heard you calling me. I had a sudden longing in me, to see you. So, I took a deep breath and pushed her away. I didn't remember anything after that. I found myself tied to a chair. No one was in the room. Suddenly I heard someone shouting my name. It was you, Liz. I saw you. But just then Mr. Miller came from behind me. He was about to open the back door and come for you and Tom. But I moved the chair a little forward and tripped him over. He fell there and because of that, even I fell. There was a knife in his pocket. I somehow took it out and freed myself and walked out the back door. I am sure you know the rest." He concluded and took a breath. "Oh Tristan! I am so sorry! If I had known all of this... I would never- He hugged me and whispered in my ear, "Look. It is no one's fault. And I know if you were there, you wouldn't have let anything happen to me. Liz... you and me... we both know that we would go to any extent to protect each other. Look, from now on, I promise to stay by your side. Forever. He let go of me. I had no words. I looked into his eyes. He understood me.

Tris opened the car door and got out. He walked to the other side and opened the door for me to step out. "GUYS! Are you done talking? For god's sake come in here and finish your *never-ending talks*!" Tom shouted from the living room. We gave each other a smirk and opened the door to a cozy living room. It had a grey leather couch, a red brick fireplace, a little round coffee table and a beautiful valley painting with flowers and a stream over the couch. I looked around and exclaimed, "It's amazing!" Tom smiled and said, "Yeah it is." Tris asked, "Whose house is this, mate?" But Tom wasn't listening. He was looking at a photo hung over the fireplace and was smiling to himself. I walked over to him and saw the picture. A man, who seemed to be in young thirties, and a woman around the same age, were standing behind a young boy who seemed to be around six. The boy was wearing a Batman costume and holding a black Labrador pup. The woman and the man were wearing what seemed to be clothing like batman's parents. I saw something written at the corner of the photo. It seemed to be written by the kid in the photo. It was a date... and... also something else. Written there was... "May 15th, 2009, 'My best birthday with mum and dad.' IS THAT TOM?!" "THOSE PEOPLE ARE NOT TOM'S PARENTS!" I was confused but I didn't want to question Tom at that moment because all three of us were tired from running around all day. I let out a sigh and asked, "Alright then, what do you want to do now?"

He looked away from the picture and suggested, "I'll show you our new home first." He showed us the kitchen first. It had a butcher block countertop and a small sink, glass shutter cabinets with dinner plates and mugs, and a small black fridge in the corner. He next showed us the bedrooms. Mine had a double bed with baby blue sheets and fluffy blue pillows. It had a round window with soft blue curtains. "This is your bedroom, Liz. I thought I'd show the house to you on your 23rd birthday. But all hell broke loose before that." Tom explained, looking out the window overlooking the yard. He took us to his room. It wasn't as big as the other one, but it was cozy. It had a single bed with a plain white sheet and a few pillows. A picture, the same as the one in the living room, was hanging above the bed. It had a window from which a bunch of dry trees could be seen. I asked, "How have you even kept this house so squeaky clean? You don't even keep your **own** house this clean." He chuckled, "Oh well, I hired a maid for that. She cleaned it every month." After seeing the house, Tris and I sat on the couch while Tom prepared dinner for us. He called us in the kitchen after about 30 minutes. As hungry as I was from all the running, I asked picking up a pot and asked, "What is for dinner?" Tom giggled, "Calm down Liz, at least get seated first. I'll go get the plates." I looked at him and ordered, "No. You sit down, and I'll go get the plates. After all, you must also be tired." "Alright fine." He agreed. I took out three dinner plates from the cabinet and set up the table. "Alright now. Let's eat." I said, leaning over to open the pot. "Um... Liz, I know you are hungry but... aren't you forgetting to bring something?" Tris asked jokingly. "Yup. Sorry. I forgot the spoons and forks." I said and got up. I opened a drawer and took out three spoons and forks. I sat down and, "NOW. Can we finally eat?" Tom nodded and opened the pot. A strong aroma reached my nose. It was my favorite. 'Spaghetti Bolognese and mashed potatoes.' I licked my lips and said, "Serve it to me first, Tom." "Alright, here." Tom said, giving me, a spoonful of mashed potatoes as I served myself spaghetti. After dinner we sat down on the couch to talk out all our tiredness. We were so busy talking that we couldn't keep track of time. "Guys, it is way past **my** bedtime. Can we discuss all this stuff later in the morning? Over breakfast?" I yawned "Alright Liz. You go sleep we'll be there in a few minutes. Alright?" Tom said, patting my head. I argued, "NO. We are all gonna go get some sleep and discuss what we are gonna do tomorrow. Over breakfast alright? "Both of them nodded and got up from the couch. Tom guided Tris and me to our bedroom. He hugged me saying, "Sleep tight, Liz. Good night." I said good night to him too and then closed the bedroom door. I was about to lie down when, "Um... are you sure we are gonna sleep in **these** clothes?" Tris asked. I chuckled, "Obviously not. I will go grab my bag from the car. And maybe ask if Tom has some clothes for you cuz you are not sleeping in **those**!" I knocked on Tom's door. He opened it and I asked for the car keys. He asked, "And why do you want the keys?" I argued (obviously, not seriously)," I am not sleeping in **these** clothes. And I will need my bag for changing them." He giggled and handed me the keys. I walked down the stairs whistling and swinging the keys on my finger. I opened the door of the house and walked towards the car. I took out my bag, looked around a little and then went back in. I walked upstairs into my room and saw that Tris had already changed into some PJ's. I went into the bathroom and came out after changing and washing off all that dirt and sweat. I then lied down on the bed. It felt as if I had laid back on a cloud. Maybe it was all that tiredness. I said good night to Tris in a sleepy voice. He giggled and then lied down too. A minute hadn't even passed, and I heard him snoring. I stifled my giggle. I was laying down for a few minutes, but I couldn't sleep. I got up from the bed and walked towards the window. I opened it and a soft cool breeze swayed across my face. I took a deep breath and looked up at the sky. The sky was clear. It was a cloudless night. The moonlight was shining softly on the swing. I smiled and remembered how I used to love swings when I was a child. I yawned. I closed the window and tucked myself in bed. I started to wind down. And before I knew it, I was fast asleep.

I opened my eyes with the sun shining bright. I heard Tom singing downstairs. He was singing a very old country song. It went something like this:

Maybe I didn't love you

Quite as often as I could have

And maybe I didn't treat you

Quite as good as I should have

If I made you feel second best

Girl I'm sorry I was blind

You were always on my mind

You were always on my mind

And maybe I didn't hold you

All those lonely, lonely times

I guess I never told you

I am so happy that you're mine...

I recognized it immediately. I knew this song. It used to be mine and Tris's favorite song and we used to start slowly dancing to its tune whenever we heard it on our T.V. I smiled and started humming to the tune of the song.

It seemed as if Tom was making breakfast. Tris was still asleep and snoring. I laughed (like a goblin) at this sight of him. It startled him and woke him up, he unfortunately fell off the bed with a loud thud. I chuckled. "Not funny, Liz. Now give me your hand. And I am hungry." I gave him my hand and got him off the floor. I went to the bathroom to freshen up. Tris knocked and came in while I was brushing my teeth. He too picked up a toothbrush and started brushing his teeth. We washed our faces and went downstairs.

As soon as we entered the kitchen, I saw the table covered in food. There was bacon and fried eggs. toasted bread, butter and jam too. "Oh, Tom! WHAT IN THE WORLD? Who the heck is gonna eat all this food?" I exclaimed sitting down on the chair. "We will be eating all of this, Liz. I cooked all of this because... never mind." Tom said piling eggs and bacon on his plate. I too grabbed bread and spread butter on it. There was something off about Tom. I wanted to ask him about the couple in the picture but couldn't build up the courage to do so. I bit a large piece out of the bread while grabbing some bacon from the tray. After filling our stomachs up to the brim, I got up and put the leftovers in the fridge. Then till afternoon I was reading a book, laying on Tris's lap while he took a nap. Yup he is always sleepy.

It was all fun and games until evening. I was sitting on the swing, in the backyard, when I heard Tris call me. I went in and before I could ask him what had happened, he panicked, "Liz! Go pack up your stuff we must leave NOW!" "But- No buts, Liz. Tom is packing some clothes for me and him. I will go grab all the water and food I can and put them in the car. You go pack up all your stuff and important things 'right.?" I hastily went upstairs. I was confused but started packing up all my stuff. I bumped into Tom as I ran out of the room. "Oh, great Liz, look, don't ask many questions. Just listen. I was looking through your purse to find your phone so I can call the police to ask what exactly was happening. Suddenly a message popped up. It was from 'NewsArc'. I opened it and started reading the article. It read something like this" he thrusted my phone in my hands and went back in his room. I read the article which read-

__People living around Brooklyn Hill Woods.__
__Please be alert and evacuate your homes as soon as__
__possible__
__As per our information, there is a huge hoard of__
__zombies attacking__
__the town on the edge of the woods.__
__EVACUATE IMMEDIATELY. THIS IS NOT A DRILL__

I followed Tom downstairs. Tristan was already waiting for us outside with bags full of food cans and water bottles. He dumped those bags in the front seat and took the bags from my hands and dumped them on the back seat. Tom thrusted his bag in Tris's hand and chuckled, "If you are gonna treat my sister like a princess then treat me like a prince too." "Yes. Your Highness" Tris joked. He dumped Tom's bag in the back seat and then shoved me in the front seat. He sat himself in the driver's seat and closed the door signaling Tom to sit in the back. He said, with a concerned look on his face, "Tom, I know you haven't slept the whole night. I saw you sitting on your bed holding that picture and crying. Here have this blanket and sleep tight." We giggled as we saw Tom snuggle in the blanket like a kitten. Tris started to drive and put on the radio. There was nothing on it but static. So, I turned it off and suggested, "Why don't we talk instead?" And we talked about this apocalyptic world, looking at the lifeless, barren road. I had a feeling that we would start a new adventure. Soon.

A NEW MATE

After almost two hours the car suddenly stopped with a jerk. Tom woke up and asked if we had reached somewhere. "Nope. We are nowhere far from Brooklyn Hill. And see the bad luck of ours, there is no more gas left in the car." I seized this opportunity, knowing we won't be going anywhere for a good few hours, and I asked Tom, "Will you care to tell us about the picture in the house?" "I'll tell you everything. But only if you don't panic." Tom promised. He took the photo out of his bag and in his hands gently stroking it with his fingers.

He started speaking, "Don't interrupt me while I tell you the truth. You can ask questions later... The truth is... I... am not the son of Mr. And Mrs. Smith. Yes, that is the name of the people who... adopted me. On the day of my sixth birthday, my real mum and dad, they... got me a puppy. And I was very happy because I had been begging them for a long time to get me a dog. Things were all good that day. They threw me a Batman themed party, invited all my friends, and had a special batmobile toy delivered all the way from Manchester. I also had a batmobile cake. It was the best birthday I ever had. After the party, my parents surprised me by dressing like Batman's parents and they even got Batman costume. My dad had rented a camera for the day, so he set it up on the cake table and clicked this photo. After clicking the photo, my mum was inside the house, cleaning the kitchen and I was playing with my dad and Willow, my new dog. My mum called my dad saying he had a call from his office. He told me he would be back in a few minutes and said that I could play with Willow near the kitchen window till he came back so my mum could keep an eye on me. I nodded and ran towards the window with Willow running besides me. Willow and I were playing fetch when I accidentally threw the stick a little too far. Willow caught the stick mid-air but fell. I was giggling and thought she was fooling me. But when she couldn't get up even after me calling her several times, I ran towards her and picked her up. Just as I was walking towards the house... something bad happened. Something I never even would've dreamed of. The house was suddenly... it was engulfed in huge flames. The neighbors came running out of their homes. I broke down then and there. I was crying bitterly.

One of our neighbors, John, held me back. The fire department was phoned. They stopped the fire from spreading, but it was too late. Mum and dad were no more. I cried, "Let go of me! I want to see mum and dad!" But John kept me from going near their bodies. An ambulance was called. It took whatever was remaining of mum and dad's bodies. After cremating their remains, I was brought back to John's house. He had a small house, and he didn't earn much. He and his wife, Kate, barely survived on the money he earned. He wanted to be my guardian, but his wife did not like his thought. That night, she gave me a pillow and blanket and told me to sleep on the couch as they only had one bedroom. She went away with a disgusted look on her face. After they were done with dinner, which she did not even **bother** to ask me to eat, she and John went to bed.

Around midnight, I woke up to Kate talking to John in a hushed, irritated voice and saying, "I do not want that scrawny little boy in our house John! We are barely surviving on the money you are earning! If we keep him in our house, how are we going to keep him alive?!" John was saying something , "Look Kate, I know we do not have much money, but Henderson has been with me through light and dark! I cannot just abandon his kid or put him in an orphanage!" "That is a great idea! Go take him to an orphanage saying you are taking him to a school and then fill in the paperwork and leave him there." I heard John shout, "You are a disgusting woman! What was I thinking when I was marrying you! You know what Kate? **You** are the one who deserves to be abandoned. Go away you witch! And never show me your ugly face again! Kate was shouting at the top of her voice now, "You are telling **me** to leave! And keeping that little rat?! FINE. I will leave. And let me tell you. You will never be happy without me!! She cursed and she opened the door. She was holding a bag and I immediately pretended to sleep. "I wish you would've also burned in the house with your selfish, ungrateful parents." I heard her mumble under her breath. She dumped the bag on the kitchen table. When she went inside her bedroom, and I heard the door close, I got up from the couch, grabbed the candle burning near the table, and lit her bag on fire. I dropped the candle in the burning bag and sneakily crept into the blanket. And a minute later I started shouting, "Uncle John! Fire! Come fast!" Kate came out first and found all her stuff burning to ashes. She was furious. I was very happy to see that look on her face. She immediately went back into the bedroom and came out with another bag with whatever other things of hers remained. And she walked out the main door making sure that we saw her make a disgusted face. Uncle John looked exhausted. He came to me and asked me, "Did you or did you not light her bag on fire?" I denied it with an innocent look on my face, "No uncle I didn't." "I know you did. But it was good. For how she treated you, I am sorry. But for lighting her bag on fire, about that, I was blind and did not see anything that happened in the last ten minutes." He joked.

In the morning, at what seemed to be 5o'clock, I heard someone coming, I kept my eyes closed. Someone opened my mouth and poured in a liquid. It was bitter. As it went down, it left my throat burning. I started feeling dizzy. I didn't remember anything after that. I woke up in the town's orphanage. I couldn't believe how cruel they were to me, after everything my dad did for them. I was in the orphanage for three years before I got adopted by Mr. Smith and his wife. And Willow, about her, I never saw her after the accident. I built this house in my mum and dad's memory when I turned 21." He concluded, "I hope you now know about my past." I saw Tom's eyes tearing up. I reached into my back pocket and pulled out a handkerchief. I handed it to Tom and sniffled, " I... I am sorry, Tom. I-

Tristan interrupted me, "Guys can we save the sentimental stuff for later? I think we got some company." We turned around and saw a crowd of people standing behind our car. It seemed as if the group was a cult or something. They were all dressed in black. A girl from the group spoke up, "If you want to save yourselves, hand us all your belongings and run-

The girl stopped mid sentence as a huge man dressed in black clothes emerged from the back of the group. As soon as he came up front, everyone bowed low to him. It seemed as if he was the leader. He started talking to Tom. I peered over Tristan's shoulder and saw that no one was looking at me. I seized that opportunity and crept towards the car. I opened my bag and took out the knife. I quietly crept back to Tris. While Tom and the Leader were arguing, I saw a man from the crowd slowly coming towards us with a bottle in his hand. I nudged Tris and nudged him to take the knife from my hand and attack the man as soon as he comes near us. He signalled to me to stay behind him. The man neared Tom. I closed my eyes out of fear. Moments later, someone grabbed my arm. I opened my eyes a little and saw Tristan, standing near me with blood on his clothes and the man's body behind his feet. I saw the people running away in different directions, into the woods. I sniffled and tried not to let my eyes tear up. Tom and I locked eyes. He came running towards me and pulled me into a hug. None of us spoke to each other for a while after the horrible incident. We were all shook.

Tris had found those weird people's vehicles and transferred that fuel into our car with a pump he found in our car. We sat there in the car and thought, 'What would become of us?' 'Where will we go?' Just as I was about to speak up, we saw smoke coming out of the car bonnet. Tris and Tom stepped out and checked it out. A few minutes later, I stepped out of the car and walked up to Tom. He looked at me, and sighed, "We're gonna have to walk from now." I was confused and asked him why. He shut the bonnet and said, "Uh... it looks like the engine oil leaked through and burnt the starting cable. So, the car won't start no matter what we do. The only option is that we walk till we find some place where we can stay safe." I nodded and immediately went to take my stuff out of the trunk. Tris and Tom followed. We started walking to the right. After almost fifteen minutes of walking, I suggested, "I don't think that walking in one direction will help us get out of the woods. Why don't we trace back our steps and reach the house? We can get an internet connection there and it will provide us will more time to think about some other place to go. Plus, we could find some tools to repair the car. That way we won't have to walk all the way through the woods." He turned to Tom agreed, "I think Liz has a point, Tom. We will be much safer inside the house than stranded inside the woods." Tom agreed and we started to trace back our steps.

After walking for almost an hour and a half, we sat down. I had almost stopped feeling my legs. Being out of breath and being tired of walking I suggested, "Why don't we rest here for a while? We can drink some water, eat something and then move ahead. Tom and Tristan fell on the ground as soon as I finished speaking. It was clear that all of us were tired. I snatched the food bag from Tris and took out some *Howlers*. These were my favorite candies because they were shaped like wolves and were cotton candy-flavored. I ate some and handed the rest to Tom. I sat down and drank some water. After around twenty minutes of snacking, we packed everything up and got up. Suddenly, we heard a gunshot. Tristan shouted, "Kneel down on the ground Liz!" I did so and closed my eyes. I felt someone grab my arm. I slowly opened my eyes and saw Tris. He signalled to me to get up and run. I grabbed his hand, and we started running. Tom also ran behind us. Whilst running, we heard another gunshot. A few minutes later, there we were, tied up, guns pointed at our heads. I was whimpering. I noticed that these were the same people who had threatened us a while ago. They were whispering something between themselves. And suddenly, something horrible happened. Again. Something that shook our soul to the core. A huge hoard of walkers attacked us. What were we gonna do? Those people were running away, and we were just there. Tied, on the ground. Thankfully, all walkers ran behind those people. I tried to get up but failed. Obviously. But a walker came running my way and suddenly, an axe came flying out of nowhere. It hit the walker's head and it fell near me. I took a sigh of relief. A minute later, a guy with a fair skin tone, wavy, messy dark brown hair, spars eyebrows, brown eyes, a grecian nose, and thin lips came running towards us. I could make out those features from a distance.Damn! I had a good eyesight. Okay. Back to the point. He introduced himself as Nathan Marshall. OH MY GOD! THIS GUY WAS MY BIGGEST NIGHTMARE! He studied with me in high school and bullied me all the time! One time, he covered my locker in pictures of Tristan and spread a rumor that I was dating him! Oh, how I wish he would have been a zombie right now and I could smash his head. With a brick. Covered in spikes and dipped in poison. Ok back to the point. He came up to me and said sarcastically, "Elizabeth Lewis. Everybody's high school crush. I am surprised you survived this long." I gave him a smirk and said, "Well, if animals like you can survive this apocalypse, so can I." "All jokes aside, I am not the same person I used to be back in high school." He claimed, looking at me. I looked at him and rolled my eyes. He asked Tom, "Look big bro. I am not the guy who I was. I have changed. Now. If you'd allow me to guide ya'll to the camp I have, then we can talk and presumably be safe." Tom agreed, for the sake of our safety. We started walking. Nathan in the front, me and Tris in the middle, and Tom at the back. While walking we encountered various dead bodies. I recognized some of them from the people who attacked us.

Nathan led us through some thick trees before announcing that we had arrived. The so-called camp had a small shelter, a small wooden structure with 'LOO' inscripted on it. The door was open and had a bucket with water and a wooden chair/toilet like thing inside, beside the shelter was a barrel, which I presumed had food, and in the shelter was a box which had bullets inside of it. He pointed towards the shelter and told us, "You guys can rest there. I'll get you some water." Tristan curtly declined and asked, "No. Thank you, we don't want YOUR water. Would you care to tell us, why did you bring us here and how did you find us?" Nathan scoffed, "Oh Tristan. You still have that same old attitude. That is why you never got anywhere." Tris looked at me and groaned, "Liz, I knew we shouldn't have followed him. But I respected Tom and did so." I signalled to him to stay quiet, and he did. Ignoring what Tristan had just said, Nathan handed us all a glass of water each. Tom drank it all in one gulp, I drank some and put it down, but Tristan, being as stubborn as he always was, did not touch his glass. Why couldn't he just forget the past and move on? Nathan asked me, "Liz, would you please come here, for a moment? I need to talk to you." I got up and started to follow him. Tristan wanted to follow but stopped when Nathan added, "**Alone**."

He took me to a corner and apologized, "Liz, I am so sorry for whatever I did to you and Tristan in high school. I was immature and didn't care about other people's feelings. I... I am sorry...Liz." I apologized, "Let's leave the past behind and focus on the present. I... am also... sorry." As soon I finished speaking, he hugged me, and I hugged him back. He broke down and I sensed that he had been holding it in for all too long. I whispered in his ear, "Shh... It will all be okay, and, after all, you have found yourself some good **new** friends." He let go, smiled and giggled, "Of course. Nothing better than settling terms with your high-school nemesis in the middle of an apocalypse." I turned to my right and saw Tristan, with a disappointed look on his face. I sighed, knowing it was no use trying to argue with Tristan. I put all the thoughts aside and smiled at Tris. He understood not to say anything.

We had found a safe shelter and Nathan had found a group of friends. And I hope he truly has changed. **I HOPE.**

CHAPTER FOUR

ON THE RUN AGAIN

It had been fifteen days since we arrived at Nathan's shelter. There was not a sign of Walkers around. With the help of Tom, Nathan and I built another shelter besides the old one. I would sleep there with Tom, and Tristan and Nathan slept in the old one. Since we arrived, I wondered why there was not a single Walker around. I did not even see a boundary wall on the way.

One evening I saw Nathan going out of the camp site. Being the curious soul I always was, I decided to follow him. Secretly.I saw many bodies of Walkers surrounding most of the other boundary of the campsite. As soon as he was a few metres away from the campsite.I took the chance and crept into the woods, maintaining my distance from him. He was walking deeper into the forest. I soon had to start jogging to keep up with him. God, couldn't he take smaller steps?! Soon we were out of the woods and on the way to a car. I did not see that car on our way here. Maybe it was a different route. He was about to drive away when I shouted, "NATHAN WALKER! STOP RI- I was so out of breath. I should hit the gym when all of this is over.

Nathan stepped out of the car and sprinted towards me. He closed the gap in between us and put his huge hand over my mouth. He whispered, "Shhh... Do you have any idea how much trouble you are gonna land us in if you keep shouting like that?!" My breath shuddered. I looked down at his hand which was still on my mouth. He understood and took his hand off. You- he cut me off and whispered, "Shh..Shh... Wait. I'll tell you everything. Just get in the car. You know what. I won't **tell** you. I will **show** you. Get in the car. Now." He grabbed my hand and started walking. I was barely keeping up with him. What was his intention? He shoved me in the front seat and slammed the door shut. He sat in the driver's seat and drove away; into the direction of the house. WHY!?

We soon reached the house. I saw hundreds if not thousands of walkers surrounding the house and woods. But they weren't going into the woods. The car was parked in between a few trees. I turned towards Nathan but found him gone. I opened the door and saw the trunk open and Nathan bent in it, searching for something. I walked towards him and, OH MY MY! In the trunk were tons of guns, ammunition, scopes, daggers, machetes and what not! Nathan saw me standing there, my eyes wide, jaw dropped from the shock. "I know what you're thinking, 'WHERE THE HELL DID *I* GET ALL OF THIS!' I could only manage to nod, still processing what all I had just seen. Nathan started, "You see, after high-school, I decided not to attend college and joined the military and after a few years of serving my country, I retired with several awards for shooting and... took over my father's mafia business." My eyes started to widen again but Nathan grabbed my wrist and mouthed the words 'not now'. He let go of my wrist and quietly closed the trunk.

He walked a few metres away from the car and placed a speaker on the top of a platform which had been made on a branch. He signalled me to go and sit inside the car. After placing the speaker and pressing a few buttons on a device he jogged back to the car and sat back in. I wanted to ask him what we were doing in a Walker filled zone and that too when the sun was about to set, but held that urge back. My little bubble of thought broke when I heard him open the door again. I asked him with a look of confusion, " Would you care to explain what is going on?!" He sighed and nodded. WHAT WAS HE DOING AND WHAT FOR?! I opened my door to step out but Nate signalled me to stay inside and press the power button on the screen. The headliner moved, to reveal glass underneath it. He climbed up on the roof and laid there on his stomach, with a gun. His shirt lifted as he laid down and I saw his lean body. WHEN THE HELL DID HE GET ABS! OK. Has to be the military training. I gulped the lump of saliva in my mouth. 'OKAY. LIZZIE. CALM DOWN. Now is not the time to think about this.' I thought to myself. Suddenly, I heard a gunshot. I looked in front of me. The windscreen was now covered in blood. I quickly got out of the car, I saw a walker, lying dead on the bonnet of the car. I looked at all the blood in horror, as Nathan climbed down. His pearly white teeth were displayed in a truimphant smile. "EXCUSE ME! You just killed someone and you are **smiling**." I bawled. "I didn't kill a person who was alive I killed a *dead* person." Nathan explained calmly. "WHAT!" I gasped. "OK. Let me explain. When a person turns into a Walker, the brain dies but not completely, the person's eyesight stops working, but their ears and smell get sharper. A craving for human flesh starts. The virus takes over the nervous system and the person starts biting other people to transfer the virus. Also when a walker or zombie is killed, they do not feel pain, as their pain receptors stop working as soon as the virus takes over the brain, and their eyes turn white. Do you understand now?" Nathan concluded. I just nodded.

Suddenly we realised that the music was not playing anymore. And because of our talking, the walkers were now walking towards us. "Shit. Shit. Shit. Shit." Nathan was muttering continuously under his breath. He signalled me to pick up the gun from the ground. I did and Nate shouted, "Fire away, Liz." "WHAT NO!" I shouted back. Nate argued, "This is no place to fight, and I will not be turning into one of *those* **today**!" "Fine." I muttered under my breath, as I loaded the gun. I took a deep breath and fired my first shot. I misses. Terribly. Now even more Walkers were coming towards us. Nate saw this and asked me from the window, "Do you know how to drive?" I nodded. He got out of the driver's seat hurriedly and came towards me. He snatched the gun from my hand and I shifted to the driver's seat. I started the car. Nathan hastily got in and asked me to drive out of the hiding place. I did so and took a sharp turn.

I drove for a few miles and then stopped the car suddenly when Nathan shouted, "WAIT!" I looked at him and asked him in an irritated tone, "WHAT HAPPENED?!" "We left your brother and **best friend** at the campsite." Nathan said with a look of concern on his face. "SHIT." I mumbled under my breath. All this while, we were so busy fighting off Walkers and saving our own lives that we forgot we had two other people who were waiting for us. 'CRAP. I hadn't even told any of them about me following Nathan. But where the HELL were they when I was going into the woods. They weren't in the shelter, or near the food barrel or bathroom.' I thought to myself. "We have to go get them!" I shouted. But Nathan was not paying attention. He was calling someone through his sattelite phone. WHAT THE-! DID HE JUST STEAL THE WHOLE MILITARY SURVIVAL PACK WHEN HE HEARD OF THE ZOMBIE OUTBREAK! Someone from the other side spoke up, "HELLO- " It was Tom. "Listen mate. It's me, Nathan. We kinda got into a situation here. So- Tom cut him off and asked hesitantly, "Is... is Liz with you?" I prompted, "Yes... Yes I am here Tom. I... I'll explain everything to you when we meet. WAIT. Where were you when I snuck into the woods to follow Nathan?" "You went into the woods. **ALONE! WITH NATHAN!**" Tristan shouted from behind Tom. "I am *still* here Tristan." Nathan said. "STOP IT, YOU GUYS!" I shouted in a frustrated tone. All three of them understood it was not to talk back. I sighed and explained to Tom, "Listen, Tom. We won't be able to come back to the camp site from this side, as we got a bit of a Walker situation there. So, all you need to do is pack up whatever food, water, clothes are there and start walking to the other side of the woods. It will take us approximately three or four hours to reach to the other side, so pack up everything now and start getting out from there as early in the **morning** as possible." I concluded. "Everything which is **ours.** Right Liz?" Tristan asked. "Yes. And by 'ours' I hope that you understood it included Nathan too." I added. I heard Tom giggle over the phone. I bid them bye and cut the call. "I guess we can sleep in the car for now. It's pretty late to drive too.

I looked at the clock shining on the car screen as it displayed '1:37AM' in bright white numbers. "I guess so." I muttered as I tried to get comfortable in the seat. I couldn't sleep with a car wheel in front of me. Nathan saw me struggling to fall asleep and grumbled, with his eyes still closed, "If you can't fall asleep we can switch. I can fall asleep anywhere when I am tired." "I think I'll go in the backseat." I suggested. He nodded and I watched as he dosed off to sleep. I queitly opened the door and went to the backseat. It hadn't even been a minute; I was about to doze off, when I hear Nathan snoring, loud. I stifled my giggle and smiled. I thought, "He had been so busy protecting me, he probably hadn't even slept in a few days." I was tired but couldn't fall asleep. The thought of Tom and Tristan being at the campsite without weapons to defend themselves, kept me awake. I took out my phone from my jacket pocket, which thankfully had a zipper to prevent things from falling, and thanks to technology the phones had been thinned down to a rod. I just had to switch it on and it projected my 'phone'. I turned it on and unlocked it. It was too bright for two in the morning so i turned down the brightness. I looked through *Memory Lane* (It was my phone's gallery) and pulled up a photo of the three of us. We were so happy back then. No worries and also no COVID or zombies. I yawned quite a few times while looking through some more pictures. So, I switched off the rod and put it in my pocket, making sure to close the zipper.

CHAPTER FIVE

THE END

I woke up when the car suddenly stopped with a jerk. I struggled to open my eyes but when I did, I saw Nathan, my head was on his lap. "Woah!" I blurted. "Oh. Good morning Liz." wished Tom. I turned my head and saw Tristan in the driver's seat and Tom in the passenger's seat. "Would you like some food?" asked Nathan, offering blueberries, as I lifted my head from his lap and sat upright. "We didn't wake you up, knowing you would shower us with questions." Tristan joked, keeping his eyes on the road. "When did **you** start driving so carefully?" I said. "Oh, well Nate warned there might be Walkers on this way." Tristan said. "*Nate,* is it?" Tom chuckled, which earned him a punch on the bicep. "Ouch." Nathan mocked him.

Two hours later, the car suddenly stopped. I looked up from my 'phone' and saw a hoard of walkers in front of the car. "RUN THEM OVER!" I shouted, panicking. "Liz, calm down." Nathan comforted, rubbing my back, as my breathing became heavy. The walkers were nearing the car, I noticed that one of them, in the front, had normal eyes. He neared the car handle, I shouted, "TRISTAN! LOCK THE DOORS!" But it was too late. The walker unlocked the door. Several walkers surrounded Tristan. I was panicking and slowly losing conciousness. The last thing I saw before becoming unconcious was hundreds of walkers, suffocating Tristan. I heard blur shouts, and grunts.

I woke up and saw blurry images of blood-covered people. I heard faint screams, pleas, and sirens. I heard someone muttering my name. I saw a glimpse of Tristan, beside me. He was covered in blood. and had a a nurse trying to cover his wound on his arm and neck. I was feeling dizzy again. I heard 'We can't save him, he's infected.' I was unconcious again.

I slowly opened my eyes. I struggled as bright white lights stung my eyes. I heard someone say, "She's Awake." I slowly opened my eyes and saw Tom. He was covered in blood from head to toe, but it seemed as if he wasn't bitten. The blood wasn't his. It... was... was- I suddenly remembered what I had seen a few minute ago or maybe hours ago. I... I had seen Tristan. WHERE WAS HE?! I frantically tried to get up but felt a hand on my shoulder, I looked up. It was Nate. I felt pain in my arm. I looked down and saw that I had been given a drip. It had been tugged a little from sudden movement. I felt my arm muscles twitching. But I didn't care about that. I wiped a tear from my cheek with my my other hand. Nathan still had his hand on my shoulder. "Nathan... NATE! WHERE IS TRISTAN? I want to see him! Please Nathan!" I broke down at the thought of Tristan being... dead. "He... Tristan... he is dead... Liz." Nathan blurted out, hugging me tightly. "We are currently at a military base camp. Nathan made some arrangements for... us." Tom said. I turned around and saw him holding a cup of tea. "YOU ARE HERE DRINKING TEA! Where is Tris!?" Take me to him, Tom! Please." I cried. Tom sighed and shaked his head. "No more, Liz." He managed to blurt out before breaking down himself.

He pulled himself together and started, "After the doors unlocked, that man you saw was infected. He too turned a few minutes later. We... we tried saving him, Liz. We truly did. He gave up his life, in an attempt to save you. Nathan had managed to fire a few shots. We got out of the car without getting bitten. We started running. I picked you up, so we could go faster. Nate was firing shots continuously. We didn't stop until we reached a safe point.That is when we saw that Tristan was bitten. We sat him down.A minute hadn't even passed when the hoard had caught up to us. Tristan made sure we were safe and stayed at the end fighting the hoard off. To give us time to run away." "But I...saw him. He was just wounded. I saw a nurse- "No you didn't. It was me. I was covering up his wounds." Nate clarified. Tom continued, "He asked us to tie him, so he wouldn't hurt us. We had no choice, Liz. We tried our best, but- "That's enough." I said. My breath shuddered. I just lost my only best friend. He gave up his life to protect us. I closed my eyes for a moment to take that all in. As I closed my eyes, I saw **him**. I saw Tristan. Our first meeting. I couldn't even bid him goodbye. He wasn't supposed to die. I opened my eyes as I felt someone take off the drip. I felt a sharp pain in my arm. But that was nothing, compared to the one in my heart. I still heard Tristan saying, " Liz, if you were there, you wouldn't have let anything happen to me." I felt as if it was all my fault.

It had been a month. Since all of it. Since Tristan died. I was feeling much better. I wasn't getting nightmares about **him** anymore. The government had made a huge eco-system in a dome. And Nathan had managed to fit us in. Thanks to his connections. We had a home there, near the hospital, since I was still prone to seizures and panic attacks.

My best friend's death had led me to PTSD. But I was better now. *He* was in a better place now. We had constructed a gravestone in the cemetery for Tristan. We decided to engrave it with-

Tristan Hillary

31/07/2016 - infinite

A best friend gone too soon

A younger brother

A saviour

We didn't write his death date because he would always be alive. In our hearts.

We Miss You. Tristan Hillary. My Best Friend.

Epilogue

It had been five years since we were living in 'The Dome'. Uncle Tom had moved out of our home and gotten married to Aunt Roisin **and** they had you. Well even I got married to someone. "Who?" my four year old twins curiously asked . I smiled and said, "It was your Dada, dumplings." Just as I said that, Nathan walked in with a cake. " Who wants cake now?" He asked. I turned around and saw a cake in his hand. Vanilla. I despised vanilla cake but... Tris loved it. He would always eat it near me and annoy me. I smiled. I had completely forgotten that it was July 31 today. Tristan's birthday. We still celebrated it after is death. Every year. But after we had the twins, we barely had time to eat lunch.

This was the first time in three years that we were celebrating his birthday. The cake had pistachios on top, with 'Happy Birthday Tristan' written on a chocolate block. I sniffled. I heard a knock on the door. I saw Tom and Roisin standing there with a paper in her hand. I snatched it from her. It read, **'Get ready to style me, Auntie Liz. -Love, your niece.**" 'Aww, Congrats, you guys!" Nate and I said in unision. I hugged Roisin and congratulated her. As they entered the house. I shot Tom 'the look' for hiding such a big news from me. My three year old twins had woken up from their nap. Nate took both of them and Angi out in the garden to play. We chatted for a while before cutting Tristan's cake together. Nate loved vanilla cake too. And it looked like he passed it on to the twins too. Ever since they turned two, Aspen and Sage loved cake. Especially vanilla. I looked at Nate and mouthed 'Thank you'. He smiled and whispered in my ear, "Anything for my family." He let go of me and planted a kiss on my forehead.

Everything was finally better. I had a loving family. I had joined the gym, and went running with Nate on the weekends.

We were in the living room, talking, when the lights suddenly went out. The alarm started blaring. I held the twins close to me. OH GOD! NOW WHAT!